Learn About

Animals

UNEXPECTED SWIMMERS

BY CLAIRE CAPRIOLI

Children's Press®
An imprint of Scholastic Inc.

A special thank-you to the Cincinnati Zoo & Botanical Garden for their expert consultation.

Copyright © 2025 by Scholastic Inc.

All rights reserved. Published by Children's Press, an imprint of Scholastic Inc., *Publishers since 1920*. SCHOLASTIC, CHILDREN'S PRESS, and associated logos are trademarks and/or registered trademarks of Scholastic Inc.

The publisher does not have any control over and does not assume any responsibility for author or third-party websites or their content.

No part of this publication may be reproduced, stored in a retrieval system, or transmitted in any form or by any means, electronic, mechanical, photocopying, recording, or otherwise, without written permission of the publisher. For information regarding permission, write to Scholastic Inc., Attention: Permissions Department, 557 Broadway, New York, NY 10012.

Library of Congress Cataloging-in-Publication Data available

ISBN 978-1-5461-0129-1 (library binding) | ISBN 978-1-5461-0130-7 (paperback)

10 9 8 7 6 5 4 3 2   25 26 27 28 29

Printed in China 62

First edition, 2025

Book design by Kay Petronio

Photos ©: cover, 1: bearacreative/Getty Images; 8–9: Thomas Marent/Minden Pictures; 11 inset, 12 inset: Martin Harvey/Getty Images; 16–17: Michael Pitts/Nature Picture Library/Alamy Images; 24–25: Suzi Eszterhas/Minden Pictures; 26: wrangel/Getty Images; 27 top: Doug Lindstrand/Design Pics/Getty Images; 29 top: Steve Woods Photography; 29 bottom: tracielouise/Getty Images; 30 top left: Denja1/Getty Images; 30 top right: by wildestanimal/Getty Images; 30 center: Nathan Derrick/Getty Images; 30 bottom left: Zocha_K/Getty Images; 32: Martin Harvey/Getty Images. All other photos © Shutterstock.

CONTENTS

INTRODUCTION: Animals That Swim 4

CHAPTER 1: Capybaras 6

CHAPTER 2: Elephants 10

CHAPTER 3: Marine Iguanas 14

CHAPTER 4: Pigs 18

CHAPTER 5: Sloths 22

MORE UNEXPECTED SWIMMERS 26

KEEP SWIMMING! 30

GLOSSARY 31

INDEX 32

INTRODUCTION
ANIMALS THAT SWIM

Can you think of some animals that swim? Fish, dolphins, and sea turtles live in water and swim. But there are other animals that swim that might surprise you. These animals come in different shapes and sizes. They live in different **habitats**.

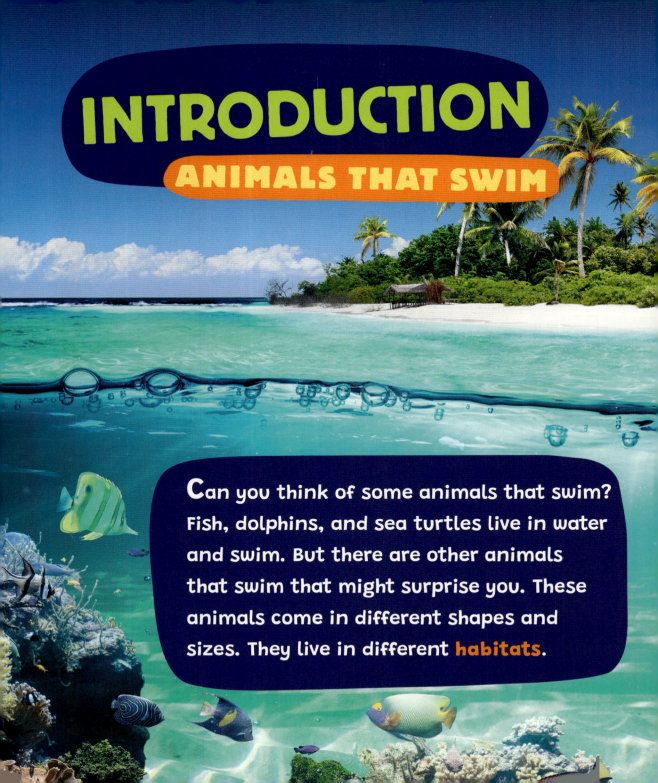

Some animals swim to cool off or hide from **predators**. Some find their food in the water. Some animals travel by swimming. Get ready to learn about some of these unexpected swimmers!

CHAPTER 1

CAPYBARAS

FACT FILE

ANIMAL GROUP: Mammal

HABITATS: Forests, Savannas, Wetlands

DIET: Herbivore

HOW BIG?

Capybaras can weigh more than 100 pounds (45 kg).

That is about the same weight as a large dog!

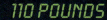
110 POUNDS

FACT! Capybaras live in groups called herds. There can be as many as 40 capybaras in a herd.

This capybara pops its head above the water plants while swimming.

Can **rodents** swim? Capybaras can! They are the largest rodents on Earth. Capybaras live near wetlands, lakes, and rivers in South America. They must swim to eat. Capybaras feed on grass and water plants. They have **webbed** feet to help them swim.

Capybaras also jump in the water to hide from predators such as jaguars. They can also spend all day in the water to keep cool. Their ears, eyes, and nostrils are high on their head.

Capybara herds usually swim together.

FACT!
When they sense danger, capybaras will bark to warn the herd.

This helps them to hear, see, and breathe while in the water. Capybaras can also swim underwater. They can hold their breath for up to five minutes!

CHAPTER 2

ELEPHANTS

FACT FILE

ANIMAL GROUP: Mammal

HABITATS: Forests, Grasslands, Savannas

DIET: Herbivore

HOW BIG?

Elephants can weigh up to 14,000 pounds (6,350 kg).

That is about as heavy as three pickup trucks!

14,000 POUNDS

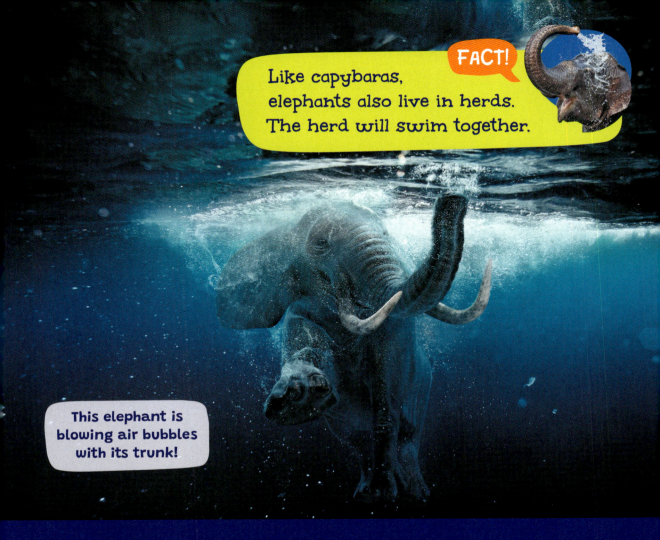

FACT! Like capybaras, elephants also live in herds. The herd will swim together.

This elephant is blowing air bubbles with its trunk!

Elephants are excellent swimmers! They swim to cool off. But how can the largest land animal on Earth swim? The fat on an elephant's body allows it to float in the water. They use their four huge legs to paddle and move. Elephants can even swim underwater with only their trunks sticking out. They use their trunks like snorkels to breathe!

FACT! There are three types of elephants: African savanna, African forest, and Asian. African savanna elephants are the largest type of elephant.

Elephants also need plenty of water for drinking and keeping cool. They suck up water in their trunks to put in their mouths to drink. Sometimes they also spray it over

These African savanna elephants are taking a cool drink of water.

their body to cool off. Elephants do not sweat. Cooling off in the water or rolling in mud protects them from the heat. They also like to play in the water, especially baby elephants!

CHAPTER 3

MARINE IGUANAS

FACT FILE

ANIMAL GROUP: Reptile

HABITAT: Oceans

DIET: Herbivore

HOW BIG?

Marine iguanas are 4 to 5 feet (1.2 to 1.5 m) long.

That is about the same height as an eight-year-old child.

* Ruler not to scale.

FACT! Marine iguanas only live on the islands in the Galápagos. Their size, shape, and color are different on each island.

The Galápagos Islands can be found off the coast of South America.

Marine iguanas must swim to survive! They get their food from the ocean. They feed on **algae** growing on rocks underwater. Like all reptiles, marine iguanas are **cold-blooded**. They cannot control their own body temperature. They need the sun to warm up before diving into the cold ocean.

Marine iguanas can dive 65 feet (20 m) underwater to get food! They are fast swimmers. Marine iguanas swim with their arms and legs tucked in. They swish their tails back and forth underwater.

FACT!

Marine iguanas sneeze out extra salt from feeding in salt water. The salt dries on their head and creates a white wig!

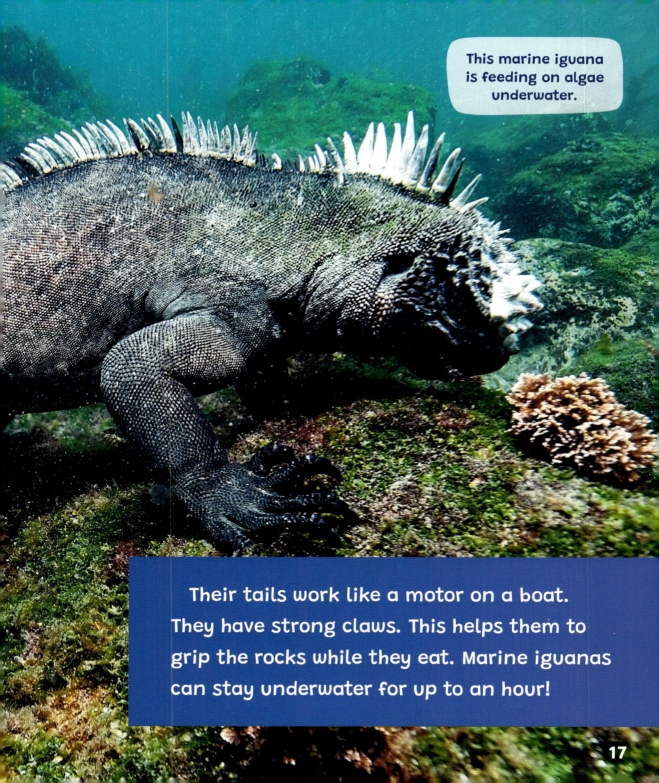

This marine iguana is feeding on algae underwater.

Their tails work like a motor on a boat. They have strong claws. This helps them to grip the rocks while they eat. Marine iguanas can stay underwater for up to an hour!

PIGS

ANIMAL GROUP: Mammal

HABITATS: Forests, Grasslands, Savannas, Swamps

DIET: Omnivore

HOW BIG?

The average pig is about 500 pounds (227 kg).

That is around the same weight as a piano.

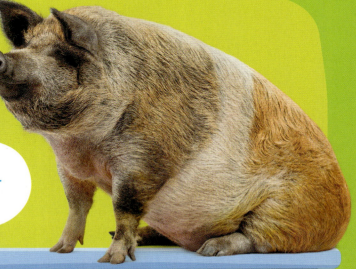

500 POUNDS

FACT!

Did you know adult pigs can run up to 11 miles per hour (18 kmh)? Most people can only run between 5 to 10 miles per hour (8 to 16 kmh).

Pigs use their legs to paddle in the water.

You might not think pigs can swim, but they can! Pigs are natural swimmers. Like elephants, pigs do not sweat. Pigs need mud or water to stay cool and protect their skin. Also, like elephants, they have a lot of fat on their body. The fat helps the pigs to float and keep their head above water.

FACT! Wild pigs will swim out of flooded areas. They can swim miles to find food or a new home.

"Pig Beach" is in the Bahamas. The Bahamas are a group of islands in the Atlantic Ocean, southeast of Florida.

Wild and **domestic** pigs can be found all over the world. Big Major Cay is a small island in the Bahamas. It is also known as "Pig Beach."

There are more than 30 wild pigs on the island. These friendly pigs will swim over to visitors in their boats in the hope of being fed.

CHAPTER 5

SLOTHS

FACT FILE

ANIMAL GROUP: Mammal

HABITAT: Tropical rainforests

DIET: Herbivore

HOW BIG?

Sloths are 2 to 2.5 feet (0.6 to 0.8 m) tall.

That is about as tall as a kitchen table.

* Ruler not to scale.

Sloths mainly feed on leaves.

FACT! Sloths only climb down from their trees once a week to go to the bathroom.

Sloths live in the rainforests of Central and South America. They move very slowly. But all sloths can swim. Why? Because swimming helps them travel between forests. Sloths spend most of their time in trees. Their long legs and curved claws help them hang from tree branches. They move slower than any other mammal.

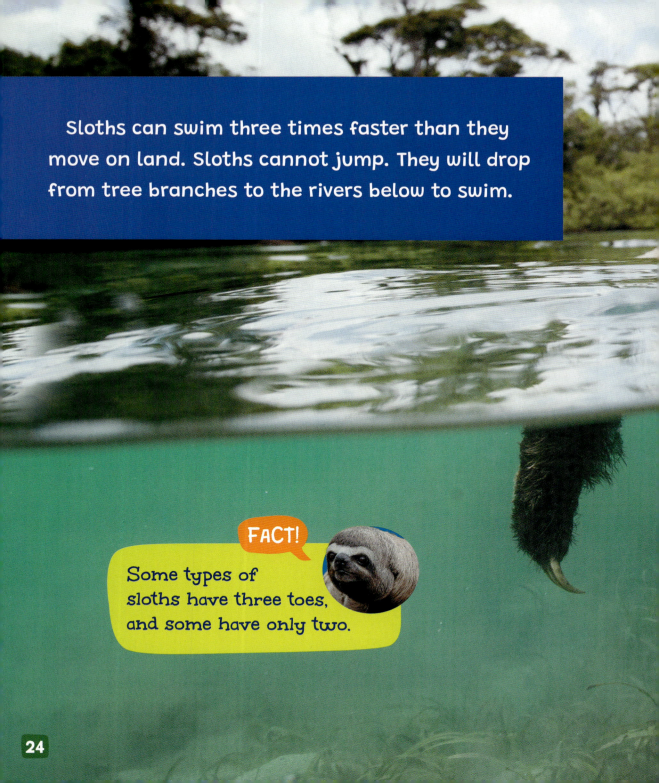

Sloths can swim three times faster than they move on land. Sloths cannot jump. They will drop from tree branches to the rivers below to swim.

FACT!

Some types of sloths have three toes, and some have only two.

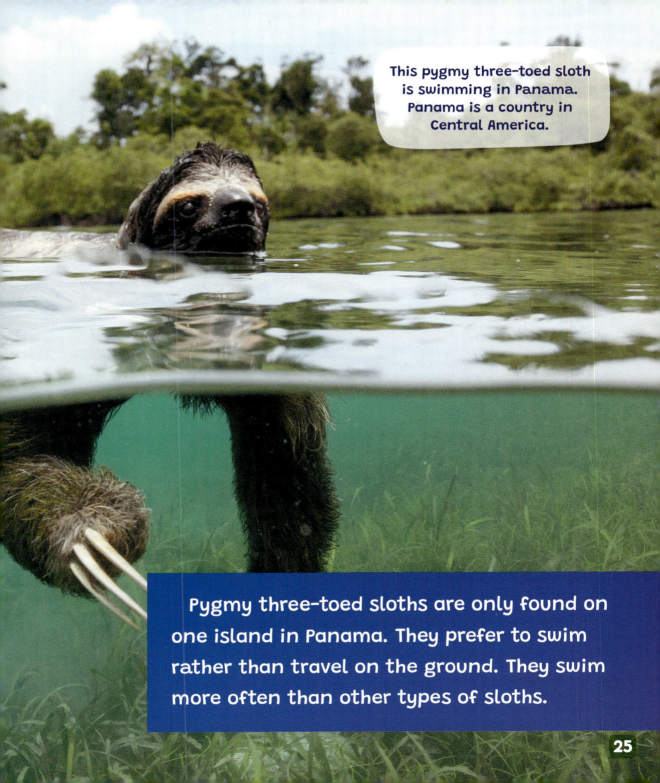

This pygmy three-toed sloth is swimming in Panama. Panama is a country in Central America.

Pygmy three-toed sloths are only found on one island in Panama. They prefer to swim rather than travel on the ground. They swim more often than other types of sloths.

MORE UNEXPECTED SWIMMERS

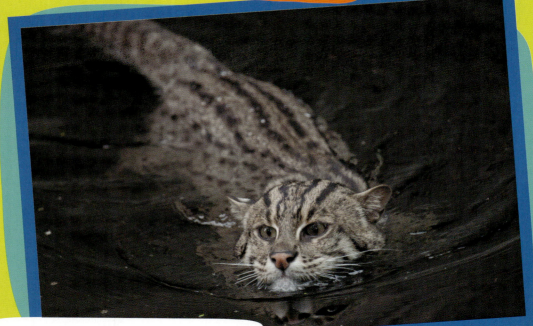

FISHING CATS

These small wild cats live in the swamps and wetlands of South Asia. Fishing cats will dive underwater to catch fish. Their ears flap down to keep water out when they dive.

MOOSE

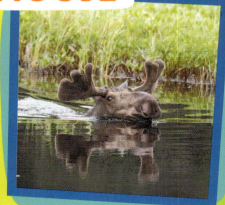

Moose can swim and hold their breath underwater for short periods of time. The water cools them off. Moose can swim about 6 miles per hour (10 kmh) for up to two hours!

COWS

Cows can swim with their long, powerful legs. In 2019, Hurricane Dorian swept three cows out to sea in North Carolina. They swam 5 miles (8 km) to get back to land.

TIGERS

Tigers are great swimmers! Their big paws are partly webbed. Tigers swim to keep cool. They can swim up to 5 miles (8 km) per hour and possibly more.

SEA WOLVES

All wolves can swim. Sea wolves swim more than other wolves. They live mainly in Canada. Sea wolves swim to get food. They eat a lot of seafood like salmon and clams.

SWAMP RABBITS

Rabbits can swim but most prefer to stay on land. However, swamp rabbits like the water. These large rabbits are strong swimmers. They live in the southern United States.

KEEP SWIMMING!

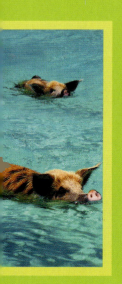

Now you have learned about some amazing animals that swim! Capybaras, elephants, marine iguanas, pigs, and sloths are all unexpected swimmers. Animals swim for different reasons. Some swim to hide or travel to new places. Swimming helps some animals survive. You can discover even more animals that swim. Visit your local zoos and aquariums. Maybe you will be surprised by what you find!

GLOSSARY

algae (AL-jee) small plants without roots or stems that grow mainly in water

cold-blooded (KOHLD bluhd-id) having a body temperature that changes according to the temperature of the surroundings

domestic (duh-MES-tik) of or having to do with animals that have been tamed

habitat (HAB-i-tat) the place where an animal or a plant is usually found

herbivore (HUR-buh-vor) an animal that only eats plants

omnivore (AHM-nuh-vor) an animal that eats both plants and meat

predator (PRED-uh-tur) an animal that lives by hunting other animals for food

rodent (ROH-duhnt) a mammal with large, sharp front teeth that are constantly growing and used for gnawing things

savanna (suh-VAN-uh) a flat, grassy plain with few or no trees

tropical (TRAH-pi-kuhl) of or having to do with the hot, rainy area of the tropics

webbed (webd) having toes that are connected by a web or fold of skin

wetlands (WET-landz) land where there is a lot of moisture in the soil

INDEX

A
arms and legs, 11, 16, 23, 27

C
capybara, 6–9
claws, 17, 23
cow, 27

E
elephant, 10–13

F
fishing cat, 26

H
herd swimmers, 7, 11

M
mammalian swimmers, 6, 10, 18, 22, 26–29
marine iguana, 14–17
moose, 27

P
pig, 18–21
pygmy three-toed sloth, 24–25

R
reptilian swimmers, 14

S
sea wolf, 29
sloth, 22–25
swamp rabbit, 29
swimming, reasons for, 5, 7–8, 11, 15, 19, 23, 26–30

T
tails, 16–17
tiger, 28
trunks, 11–12

W
webbed feet and paws, 7, 28

ABOUT THE AUTHOR

Claire Caprioli loves learning about animals and writing for kids! You can learn more about her by visiting clairecaprioli.com.